Take Me to Lǎolao

Written by **Kelly Zhang**

Illustrated by **Evie Zhu**

Quill Tree Books
An Imprint of HarperCollinsPublishers

On the night of the Lantern Festival,
the first full moon of the Lunar New Year
peeked inside Lili's house.

Earlier that evening, Lili and her family had gathered around the big kitchen table, eating bowls of pearly yuánxiāo, solving fun riddles, and making paper lanterns.

Lili was exhausted. But before she'd drifted off to sleep, she had thought longingly about Lǎolao, who was not at the table tonight.

As Lili slept, fuzzy vines slowly sprouted from the floor and snaked out the bedroom window.

"Wake up," the Moon whispered into Lili's ears. "Your lǎolao is waiting for you."

"Lǎolao?" Lili sat up and rubbed her sleepy eyelids.

When she saw the giant vines, Lili's eyes sparkled. *Will they take me to Lǎolao?*

Lili landed in her backyard, where a crystal clear
stream danced upon mossy rocks.

On the moonlit waters sat a small fishing boat,
just like the ones docked by Lǎolao's house in her
seaside village.

"Can you take me to my lǎolao?" Lili asked.
"I haven't seen her since last year's Lantern
Festival. I miss her so much."

"I'm sorry. I don't know where your
grandmother is," the boat replied. "But I can
take you to the Dragon King of the East Sea."

The Dragon King? Lili wondered. Then she remembered something Lăolao had once told her: When fishers were lost at sea, they would always ask the Dragon King for help. So Lili climbed into the boat. A gentle breeze pushed them downstream.

They sailed past mountains high and low, valleys lush and barren, forests crowded and quiet.

Finally, the boat announced, "We have arrived! The Dragon King's palace is here at the bottom of the sea."

Lili sniffed the salty air and peered down. Dark waves rose like hungry fish.

Two summers ago, Lili had snuck out of Lăolao's house to play on the beach. As the tide came in, she found herself neck-deep in water. Luckily, Lăolao rescued her before the waves swallowed her up. And she gave Lili a special necklace to keep her safe.

Lăolao, I'm not afraid of the sea anymore. Lili took a giant breath and dived in.

Down Lili swam until she found the Water Crystal Palace of the Dragon King.

"Who goes there?" the shrimp guard asked.

"I'm Lili. I wish to see the Dragon King."

"And where is your invitation?" he demanded.

"Invitation?" Lili glanced around, bewildered.
Just then, the pearls around her neck began to glow.

"Dragon's Pearls!" The guard gasped. "Honored
guest of the King, please come in."

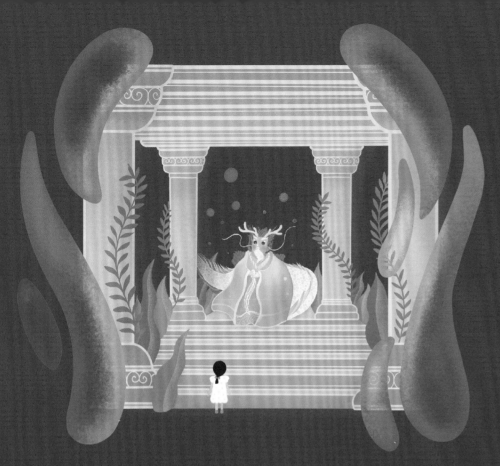

Water parted as Lili walked into a dazzling hall, where the Dragon King sat looking regal.

Lili bowed. "Oh wise King of the East Sea, can you take me to my lǎolao?"

"A human girl with Dragon's Pearls?" The king sounded amused. "I'm afraid I don't know where your lǎolao is."

Lili's heart sank. "Then who else can help me?"

"Try the Jade Emperor." The Dragon King stroked his wiry whiskers. "He is the ruler of the whole universe. He knows everything."

Lili's face lit up. "How do I find the Jade Emperor?"

"He lives in the Celestial Palace above the clouds. Give me your most precious thing and I will gladly take you there."

My most precious thing? Lili's hand drifted toward her pearl necklace.

The Dragon King nodded his approval.

No! Lili shook her head in panic. *But if I don't do it, I might never see Lǎolao again.*

Slowly, Lili loosened the delicate pearls and handed them over.

The Dragon King swiftly transformed into a magnificent blue dragon, and Lili climbed onto his back. Together they soared through water and air, past layers of misty clouds, until they reached the Celestial Palace.

Graceful fairies danced and sang to the sweet melody of flutes, harps, and bells.

"Walk up those steps and you will find the Jade Emperor," the Dragon King instructed. "Oh, and you may have your necklace back."

Lili gasped. "Thank you."

"My, my, you do look like the little girl I gave these pearls to years ago." With a sly wink, the Dragon King disappeared.

Lili climbed the giant marble steps until she reached a magnificent throne.
She bowed deeply before the Jade Emperor, with posture so perfect it
would surely have made Lǎolao proud. "Your Majesty, will you take me to my
lǎolao, please?"

"I can show you the way. But first, you must solve my riddle," the Jade
Emperor said solemnly. "Is it a wandering star or a floating lantern?
Its flame burns brightly in rain and in wind."

Lili had heard this one before! Lǎolao taught it to her on their way to last year's lantern market. Every time Lili correctly solved a riddle, she won a cute toy or a tasty treat from one of the market stalls.

What's the answer to this riddle again? "It's a . . . a firefly!" The Jade Emperor smiled and nodded. Then he dusted off his golden robe. "Let my stars be your guide."

A bridge of glittering stars spread across the sky.
Lili skipped along the celestial bridge, humming the lovely tunes the fairies had taught her.
At the end of the bridge, hundreds of lotus lanterns bobbed like orange balloons.
Lili grabbed the biggest lantern and sailed into a bustling night market.

All around her, people were celebrating the Lantern Festival. And to Lili's surprise and delight, the market looked just like the one she'd visited in Lǎolao's village!

The scents of sweet rice balls and crispy sesame pancakes tickled Lili's nose.

糖葫蘆

Lili's feet bounced over cool, mossy cobblestones.
She danced and twirled, round and round . . . right
into a dazzling lantern parade.

Boats of all shapes, flowers of all colors, fairies in rainbow dresses, animals small and great . . . and, of course, dragons. Lantern dragons that looked almost as magnificent as the Dragon King!

But where is Lǎolao? Lili searched up and down, left and right.

Clutching her pearl necklace, she felt a heaviness growing inside her chest.

Am I really in the right place? What if I never find Lǎolao? Hot tears began to swell in Lili's eyes as she swam through the jubilant crowd.

Just as she turned the corner onto the next street, Lili spotted someone sitting by the stone bridge.

Lili's heart soared—she knew who it was right away.

"Lǎolao!"

The elderly woman turned around. Her hooded eyes lit up like a million stars.

Lǎolao folded Lili into her warm arms. "My little Lili
has grown so tall! I barely recognize you."
"Lǎolao, I missed you so much. I came to find you!"
"My bǎobèi, I missed you too!"

"I want you to have this. . . ." Lili fumbled inside her pocket and pulled out a folded paper object. "Look, I made this lotus lantern all by myself!"

"How beautiful!" Lăolao's thin lips curved into a smile as bright as a crescent moon. "I will treasure it forever."

Snuggling close, Lǎolao and Lili looked up together at the shimmering night sky.

"Lǎolao, I wish I could see you every day."

"My bǎobèi, I think about you all the time." Lǎolao gently stroked Lili's hair. "And each time I think of you, I send a lantern star into the sky. Look—how many stars are there now?"

Lili started to count . . . and her eyelids soon grew heavy with sleep. "Time for bed, my bǎobèi," Lǎolao gently whispered. "Don't forget, whenever you miss me, just look into the night sky. My lanterns will always be there, watching over you, lighting your way."

All through the quiet night, a blanket of moonbeams wrapped around Lili. Warm and snug, just like Lǎolao's hug.

Author's Note

This story is inspired by my own experiences growing up as the child of Chinese immigrants in North America. My grandparents lived in mainland China all their lives. My mother wanted me to stay in touch with my grandparents and continue to learn the Chinese language and culture, so she sent me back to China each summer. Visiting my grandparents during the summer break became a family ritual, and a highlight of my year.

I had a particularly strong bond with my lǎolao (姥姥, maternal grandmother), who had taken good care of me since I was a baby. Before I could talk or walk, Lǎolao would entertain me with all kinds of funny and fantastical tales, lull me to sleep with soothing folk songs, and show me how to take care of animals and plants around the house.

During the Lantern Festival—my favorite holiday of the year—Lǎolao always made sure I had an extra-amazing time. She would feed me delicious rice balls, take me to the night market to watch the lantern parade, teach me how to solve riddles, and buy me tons of snacks and toy lanterns. Those joyful memories are still fresh in my mind, as if they only happened yesterday.

Sadly, my lǎolao passed away several years ago. I long to see her one last time. As the COVID-19 pandemic and the ensuing conflicts and disasters ravage our world, children and families everywhere are forced into heart-wrenching separations, whether temporary or permanent. I feel you, and my heart goes out to you. I hope and pray that all the folks around the world who are waiting to be reunited can soon share a warm hug again.

I wish to dedicate this story to my beloved lǎolao, and to all the grandmas who love generously, give selflessly, and live fearlessly.

Celebrating the Lantern Festival (元宵节, Yuánxiāo jié)

The Lantern Festival, also known as Yuánxiāo jié or Shàng yuán jié (上元节), marks the first full moon of the Chinese solilunar calendar and the last day of the fifteen-day Lunar New Year festivities. The Lantern Festival was first celebrated during the Han dynasty in China, which dates back more than two thousand years.

According to tradition, families would gather around a large round table and feast on bowls of glutinous rice balls (汤圆, tāngyuán) and other delicious food. The pearly white, chewy, and slightly sticky tāngyuán are stuffed with different kinds of sweet fillings, like red beans, peanut butter, or sesame paste. The roundness of the rice balls is like the roundness of the family table and the shape of the full moon. Eating rice balls symbolizes people's wishes for social harmony, family unity, and personal fulfillment.

Other activities enjoyed during the Lantern Festival include making paper lanterns, guessing the answers to riddles, going to the lantern parade, watching dragon or lion dances, and moon-gazing. Walking across a bridge can also be part of festival traditions in certain parts of China. It represents the wish to leave behind bad luck and to start on a fresh footing for the new year.

Chinese Mythological Figures and Symbols

There are many parts of Chinese mythology and folklore that show different magical creatures and colorful deities, including:

The Dragon King (龙王, Lóngwáng)

Unlike the winged, fire-breathing dragons in western stories, Chinese dragons have the power to control water and rainfall. Dragons are usually kind creatures that bring protection and good fortune to the common folk. They have been beloved and revered by Chinese people for ages, and have become the symbols of many emperors, kings, and royal households.

The Dragon King is often shown as an old, bearded man with the face of a dragon and the body of a human. He is the king of dragons. The Dragon Kings of the Four Seas are mentioned in classic Chinese fantasies. Each Dragon King rules over one of the four directional seas: East, South, West, and North. The Dragon King of the East Sea is believed to be the wisest and most powerful.

Dragon Kings are said to live in underwater palaces made from dazzling crystals, radiant pearls, colorful corals, and precious gemstones. In addition to being the leaders of their own dragon clans, the Dragon Kings also command sea creatures like fish, shrimp, and crabs.

Fishers pray to the Dragon King for protection against storms and for a bountiful catch. Farmers pray for good weather and timely rainfall to grow and harvest their crops, especially during times of drought or flood.

The Jade Emperor (玉帝, Yù dì)

The Jade Emperor is the ruler of heaven and the leader of all celestial gods. He tries to keep law and order in the universe. He often helps people who are poor and punishes those who are evil and corrupt.

It is believed that during Lunar New Year, the Jade Emperor sits on his throne to listen to prayers and requests from humans. He grants as many wishes as possible and offers pardons to those who confess their wrongdoings.

Here is one version of the folktale, which explains the origin of the Lantern Festival:

Once upon a time, the Jade Emperor's favorite pet falcon flew down to Earth and was accidentally killed by a human hunter. The Jade Emperor was very angry, and he decided to punish the humans by sending down a great fire on the fifteenth night of that year. The Jade Emperor's daughter secretly informed humans of her father's plan. To escape this punishment, humans lit torches, lanterns, and fireworks to try to fool the Jade Emperor into thinking that Earth was already burning. Since then, on the fifteenth night of each new year, folks continue to light lanterns in celebration of being spared from punishment, and to ward off bad luck for the coming year.

The Lotus Flower (莲花, Liánhuā)

Lotus flowers are the symbols of purity and holiness in the Buddhist religion. In Chinese culture, the white lotus flower is the representation of Guanyin (观音菩萨, Guānyīn púsà), the beloved goddess of mercy and compassion. Guanyin has a special soft spot for humans, and would frequently visit Earth to perform acts of kindness.

In Buddhist traditions, making a paper lotus or lighting a lotus lantern symbolizes mourning the loss of a loved one, honoring their memories, and finding peace and enlightenment.

Craft Activity: How to Fold a Paper Lotus Lantern

Easy paper lotus craft:

1. Prepare three square pieces of paper, two pink and one green.
2. Take a pink square, fold it diagonally to make a large triangle, and then fold it in half to make a smaller triangle.
3. Draw a scalloped line midway across the pink triangle (see graphic) and cut out the center portion. This is the first layer of lotus petals.
4. Take the second pink paper square and repeat steps 2 and 3.
5. Take the green square and fold it the same way you did in step 2.
6. Draw a curved line near the long edge of the folded green triangle (see graphic) and cut away the corners. This will open up to become the lotus pad.
7. Lay the two lotus petal layers on top of the lotus pad. Glue them together or thread a pipe cleaner through the center. Now you have a pretty paper lotus!

You can also try this:

- Experiment with different materials and textures for the lotus craft. What about a lotus made from felt or tissue paper?
- Pastel-colored gradient papers can make a more realistic-looking flower.
- Decorate the center of the flower with gold glitter glue or string some yellow beads on a pipe cleaner to make the lotus pod.
- If you are crunched for time, try using a green cupcake liner or paper plate as the lotus pad.

Do you have any other ideas? You can use your imagination to create!

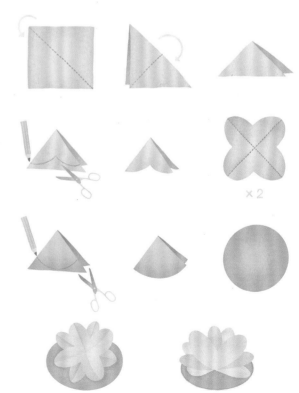

To my lǎolao, Han Huayun (韩华云),
and to all the grandmas in this world whose love lights our way
—KZ

To my beloved lǎolao, who wove enchanting celestial
tales in my summer nights of childhood
—EZ

Quill Tree Books is an imprint of HarperCollins Publishers.

Take Me to Lǎolao
Text copyright © 2024 by Yong-Li Zhang
Illustrations copyright © 2024 by Evie Zhu
All rights reserved. Manufactured in Italy.

Library of Congress Control Number: 2022946863
ISBN 978-0-06-321765-2

The artist used digital canvas to create the digital illustrations for this book.
Typography by Rachel Zegar
23 24 25 26 27 RTLO 10 9 8 7 6 5 4 3 2 1

First Edition